Dedication

This book is dedicated to my parents:
Charles and Kim.
To my siblings and nephew, who are always in
support of my creative pursuits.

Love,
Charlene K. Thomas

Published in association with
Bear With Us Productions

First paperback edition published 2021
New York,NY

Edited by Shawnon Corprew
Illustration by Martynas Marchius
Book design by Luisa Moschetti

Library of Congress Control Number:
2021908875
ISBN 978-0-578-90944-8 (paperback)

Published by Charlene K. Thomas

www.justbearwithus.com

Illustrated by
Martynas Marchius

Lena's First Trip To The Hair Salon

Written by
Charlene K. Thomas

Do you know what today is?
It's a special day.
It's my first trip ever to the hair salon!

Yep! I'm so **excited**.

I've been counting the days until Saturday,
and I've told all of my friends about it.

They are happy for me, too. A lot of the girls in
my class go to the salon whenever their moms
need a break from doing their hair.

My best friend, CeCe, has her hair done at the salon every two weeks, and she shows off her new hairstyles all the time.

Sometimes, she gets it braided
in all kinds of fancy patterns with beads.

And sometimes, she has it done with
two buns and a cute bang with a bit
of fun colors, like pink and purple!

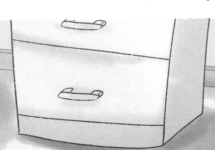

CeCe tells me that the salon is a fun place to visit.

I always wear my hair in **two twisted pigtails** on both sides of my head with **pretty barrettes**, or these **little fancy bubble balls** that my mom likes to use.

I wear them in different colors to match my school outfits.

Sometimes, Mom switches up my hairstyle to big hair puffs, but for a change, **I just want to have my hair done at the salon** like my friend, CeCe.

I asked my mom every week if she could take me
to the salon, but she told me all the time,
"Someday, Lena, I will take you. Just be patient."

So, I asked her again five days ago, and she said,
"**Yes**, Lena, I made an appointment.
You are going to the hair salon this Saturday!"

"Yay, finally!
I wonder what it will be like at the salon!"
I shouted.

Mom has been going to Ms. Gladys' Hair Salon since she was a little girl.

My nana would take Mom to the hair salon for special occasions, like **her birthday** or before **Christmas**.

Other times, Nana did Mom's hair at home, just like Mom does mine.

Every Saturday morning, Mom styles my hair.
I sit on this big, soft pillow on the floor between her
knees while she combs and brushes my hair into the two
pigtail twists with the fancy barrettes on the ends.

Mom always tells me that my hair is my crown and glory.

I start to think of all the styles I can choose from
when I get to the hair salon.

Whatever I decide, I'm sure it will look nice
and pretty because Mom says **Ms. Gladys** is the
best hairdresser in the neighborhood!

"Lena, are you ready to see Ms. Gladys?" Mom asked.
"Yes, Mom. I'm so excited!" I yelled.
"Alright, **babycakes**, let's go!" Said Mom.

"Mom, how much longer do we have to walk?" I asked.
"Just one more block and around the corner," Mom said.

"Here we are, Lena! The one and only
Ms. Gladys' Hair Salon!"
Mom said.

"Let's go in, Mom!"
I said while jumping up and down.

"You first!" Mom said.

Mom and I walk in and have a seat until it's my turn to have my hair done by Ms. Gladys.
Mom says **the salon gets very busy on Saturdays.**

There are other ladies and girls waiting to have their hair done, too. Some are sitting under the hair dryers, and others are reading books and magazines until they are called.

There's a lot of talking and laughing in the salon. I also hear music playing, sounds of the hair dryers, and phones ringing. The salon smells like **hairspray and strawberry shampoo**!

Mom says visiting the salon is a tradition.
The ladies come to the salon to have their hair done, meet with friends, and relax.

While I wait to sit in Ms. Gladys' chair, the shampoo lady takes me to the sink to wash my hair really well. **My hair looks like a great, big cloud of bubbles and suds!**

After my shampoo, the lady takes me to sit under the hair dryer. Then, we wait just a little bit more... I'm tired of waiting for my turn, but **Mom tells me to be patient.**

Just a few more minutes to go, and then, finally, **Ms. Gladys calls me to the hair chair!**

She pushes this button on the chair that sends me up a little high. Then, she places a special cover in front of me to keep my clothes clean while she does my hair.

"Now, little Lena, welcome to my hair salon!
What hairstyle do you have in mind on this fine day?"
Ms. Gladys asked me.

"Well, Ms. Gladys, I'm not quite sure!" I said.

"Oh, no worries! We can make it flow like a river, Swirl with curls, Make it into a bow, Braids with bangs... all kinds of things!

The styles are endless!
That's the beauty and magic of hair," said Ms. Gladys.

"How about bright and fluffy, like **cotton candy**?!"
I said to Ms. Gladys.

"Sure, sweetheart! All we need is a little teasing here
and there, and my special unicorn color spray,"
said Ms. Gladys.

"Let's try it!" I said.

"Well, Lena, what do you think about it?"
Asked Ms. Gladys.

"Oh, goodness, Ms. Gladys, this is pretty fun looking,
just like cotton candy! Hmm... but maybe we should
save this style for my birthday?" I asked.

"Alright, would you like to see it flowy?"
Ms. Gladys asked.

"Okay! I've never worn my hair straight before," I said.

"So, Lena, tell me what you think of this style.
A bit different from your usual style, but just as lovely!"
Ms. Gladys said.

"Mmmm... this is okay, too, Ms. Gladys.
Oh my, I can't decide.
Maybe I'll wear it standing high or very low.
I just don't know!" I said with a frown.

"Chile, don't get yourself in a frenzy bunch!
I have just the perfect style," said Ms. Gladys.

"Tell me, tell me!" I begged.

"This style is what all the little girls love.
As a matter of fact, your mother would ask for this very
style when she was your age, too," said Ms. Gladys.

"Ms. Gladys, are you talking about
the Shirley Temple curls?" Mom asked.

"Yes! Why, Lena, your mother just adored herself some
Shirley Temple curls! She couldn't stop staring in the
mirror. She always said wearing her hair in those curls
made her feel extra special," Ms. Gladys said.

"My, how I miss those curls! I wore my hair in those Shirley Temple curls on my first day of school back in the day. Honey, you couldn't tell me anything. I knew that I looked beautiful!" Said Mom with a laugh.

"Okay, I'll have the Shirley Temple curls too,
just like Mom.
I want to look just as beautiful as she is,"
I said to Ms. Gladys.

"Lena, you'll always be beautiful, no matter what hairstyle you choose,"
Ms. Gladys told me.

"That's right!" Mom agreed.

"Well, alright, let's get to the curls, girls! Maybe we can add a beautiful tiara barrette for extra razzle dazzle!" Said Ms. Gladys.

"Ta-da! All done.

It looks like this will be your favorite hairstyle," said Ms. Gladys.

"You bet! **I LOOOVVE it!** Just wait 'til all my friends see my new hairstyle. They're going to think I'm a big girl. How do I look, Mom?!" I asked.

"Babycakes, you look just like sunshine!" Said Mom.

"Thanks, Mom!"

I said with a smile.

"Well, Lena, you finally had your hair done.
We'll come back for your birthday, okay?" Said Mom.

"Okay, Mom. Thank you, Ms. Gladys.
I can't wait to come back!" I said.

"You're welcome, sweetheart," said Ms. Gladys.

"In the meantime, **we'll have to roll your hair at night
so that your curls can stay nice and bouncy,**"
Mom said.
**"Lena, your hair is like a flower. If you water it
and take good care of it, it will flourish and grow
healthy,"** Ms. Gladys said.
"Oh, and of course, always remember...
Your hair is your crown and glory!"

About the Author

Charlene K. Thomas has a professional background in media and early childhood education.

She holds a B.A. degree in Mass Communications from Cheyney University of Pennsylvania, and is a proud member of Alpha Kappa Alpha Sorority, Inc. During her downtime, she enjoys traveling, D.I.Y. crafting, reading, cooking, and family time. She currently resides in New York City.

Lena's First Trip to the Hair Salon is her debut children's book.